TOTALLY AWESOME
MAZES AND PUZZLES

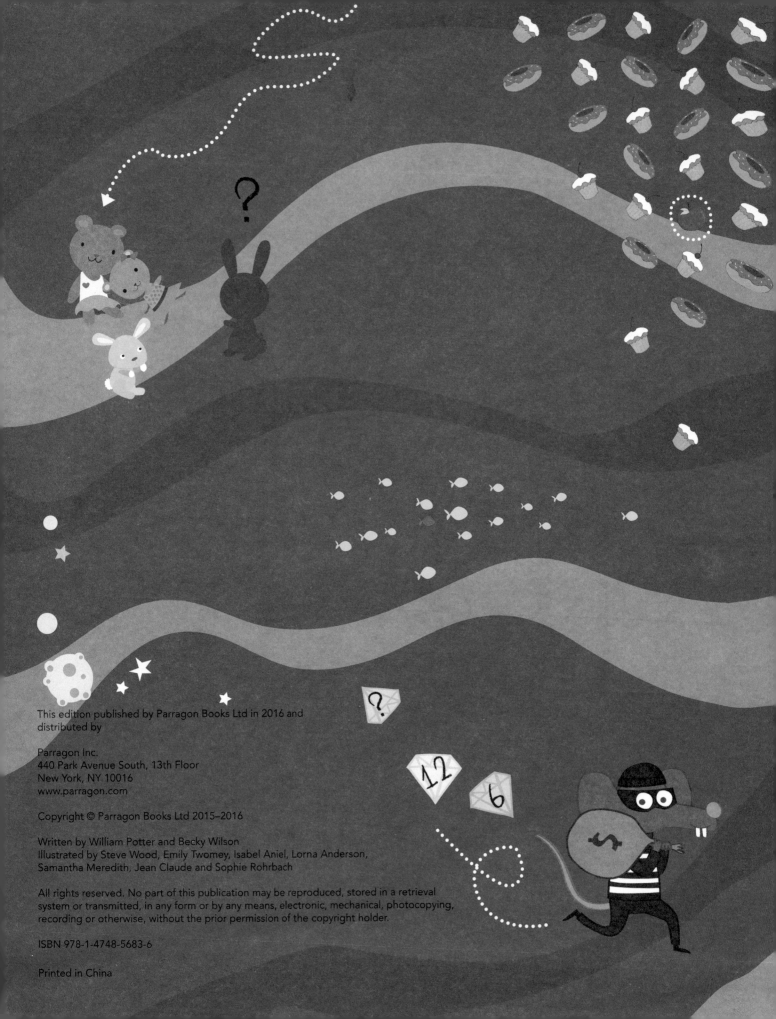

This edition published by Parragon Books Ltd in 2016 and distributed by

Parragon Inc.
440 Park Avenue South, 13th Floor
New York, NY 10016
www.parragon.com

Written by William Potter and Becky Wilson
Illustrated by Steve Wood, Emily Twomey, Isabel Aniel, Lorna Anderson, Samantha Meredith, Jean Claude and Sophie Rohrbach

ISBN 978-1-4748-5683-6

Printed in China

a b c

TOTALLY AWESOME
MAZES AND
PUZZLES

Over 200 incredibly puzzling activities

PaRragon

Bath • New York • Cologne • Melbourne • Delhi
Hong Kong • Shenzhen • Singapore

Tech teacher

The school computer has caught a virus! It keeps repeating letters. Cross out all the letters that there are more than one of to see today's subject.

C	O	Z	J	B	S	Z	O	J	Z
A	F	O	B	J	F	J	H	O	B
F	B	M	F	O	J	B	C	Z	O
J	Z	C	Z	B	Z	O	B	S	C
O	C	F	B	F	O	F	Z	O	Z
Z	B	J	O	T	Z	C	B	F	C

Today's lesson is

....

Sleepy Puppy

Dozy the dog is dreaming of his favorite part of the rug. See if you can find it!

Big brother, Little brother!

I'm Little Liam. Copy me one square at a time into the larger grid to see what my big brother Giant Jake looks like!

Tool trouble

Peter the plumber has dropped his wrenches! How many of each color are in the pile?

Green ☐

Orange ☐

Blue ☐

Pink ☐

Purple ☐

Math mystery

6 ☐ 6 = 12

15 ☐ 5 = 10

6 ☐ 3 = 9

12 ☐ 5 = 7

4 ☐ 3 = 7

Help me finish the sums by filling in the missing + and − signs.

Lost City

Follow the directions to discover the Lost Jungle City! Where is it on the map? Mark it by drawing an X.

1. From the Start, go up 4 squares.
2. Move 5 squares toward the Thorn Forest.
3. Go up 3 squares, then 2 squares right, then up 2 squares.
4. Go 2 squares toward the Pitless Bottom.
5. Move down 1 square, then left 4 squares.
6. Go down 6 squares.
7. The Lost Jungle City is 4 squares right of here!

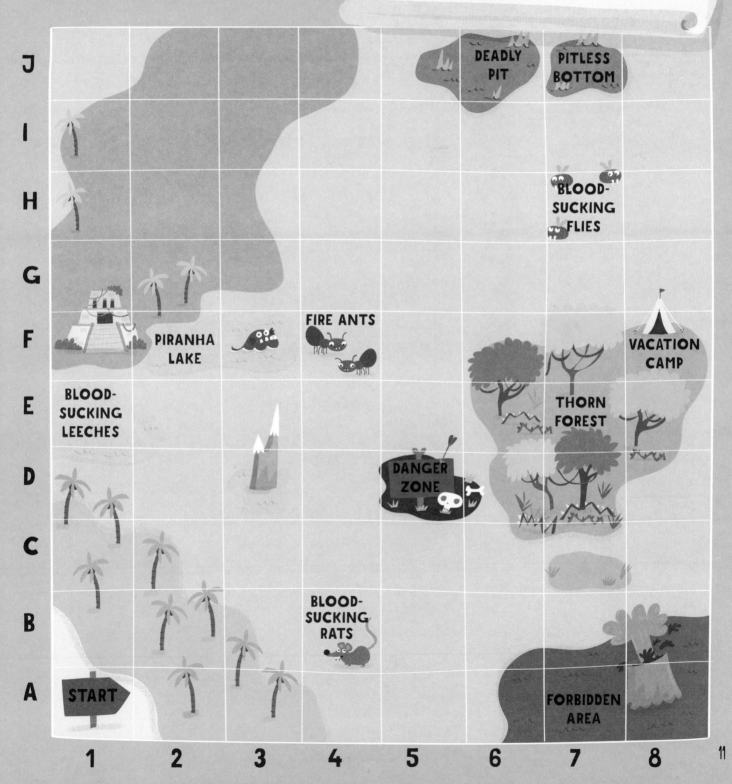

Ella is doing a survey of the coral reef...

Help her find:

10 shells

9 crabs

8 seahorses

7 shrimp

6 clownfish

5 butterfly fish

4 moray eels

3 trumpet fish

2 octopuses

1 lost diver's mask

Alien attack

Uh-oh! The aliens are planning an attack!
Color in the dotted shapes to find out
which planet they plan to strike.

vacation halves

I've been on so many vacations I can't remember where I've visited!
Fill in the stickers with the names of all the places I've been by joining two word halves from below.

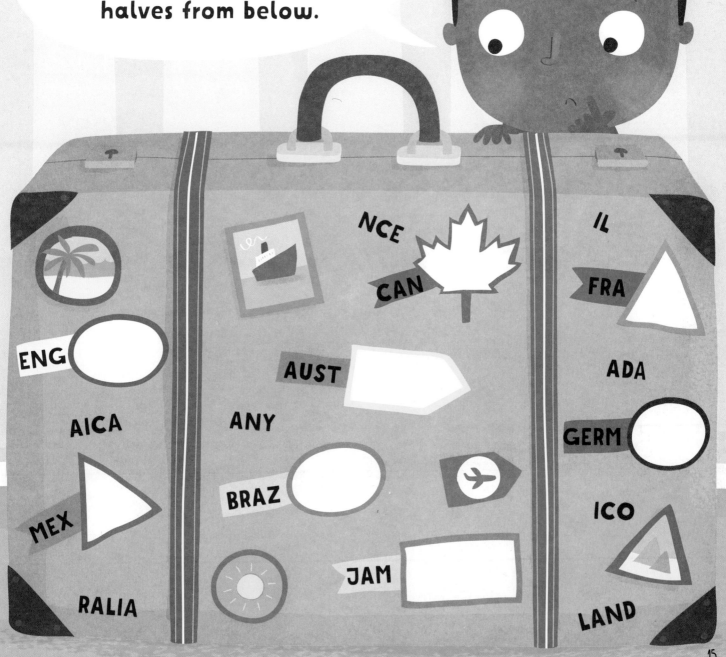

Each of these words has an opposite. Draw lines to join the pairs of opposite words.

SLOW   YOUNG

COLD

LIGHT   DRY

DIRTY

WET   TALL

FAST

HOT   HEAVY

SHORT   OLD   CLEAN

missing toppings!

Each pizza topping has a number value from 1 to 5. Draw toppings onto slices 2, 3, and 4 to make the toppings on each slice add up to exactly the same number as slice 1.

Monster change

Dr. Jangle drank a potion that turned him into Mr. Hideous! Order the pictures from 1 to 9 to see the change.

Copy street

Mr. Mirror wants his house to look exactly like his neighbor's.

He has everything he needs to build it, but which THREE parts does he NOT need?

This monster ate the menu!

Cross out all letters that appear twice, then unscramble the rest to see what he's ordered.

J M U S
C A E J
C K M
U S

Now quickly draw it here—before he eats the table!

Happy

Birthday

Silly Circus

It's audition time at the
Superstar Circus! Can you find:

9 balls	5 red noses
9 yellow stars	4 juggling pins
8 saucers	2 buckets
6 hoops	2 giant shoes
10 cups	1 rabbit

shadow star

This singer is in the spotlight,
but which shadow matches her exactly?

Penguin puzzle

Hop this little penguin home across the different-shaped icebergs in this order:

① 1 ② 2 ③ 3 ④ 4

You can go vertically or horizontally but not diagonally.

Start!

Home →

Finish!

Bird spotting

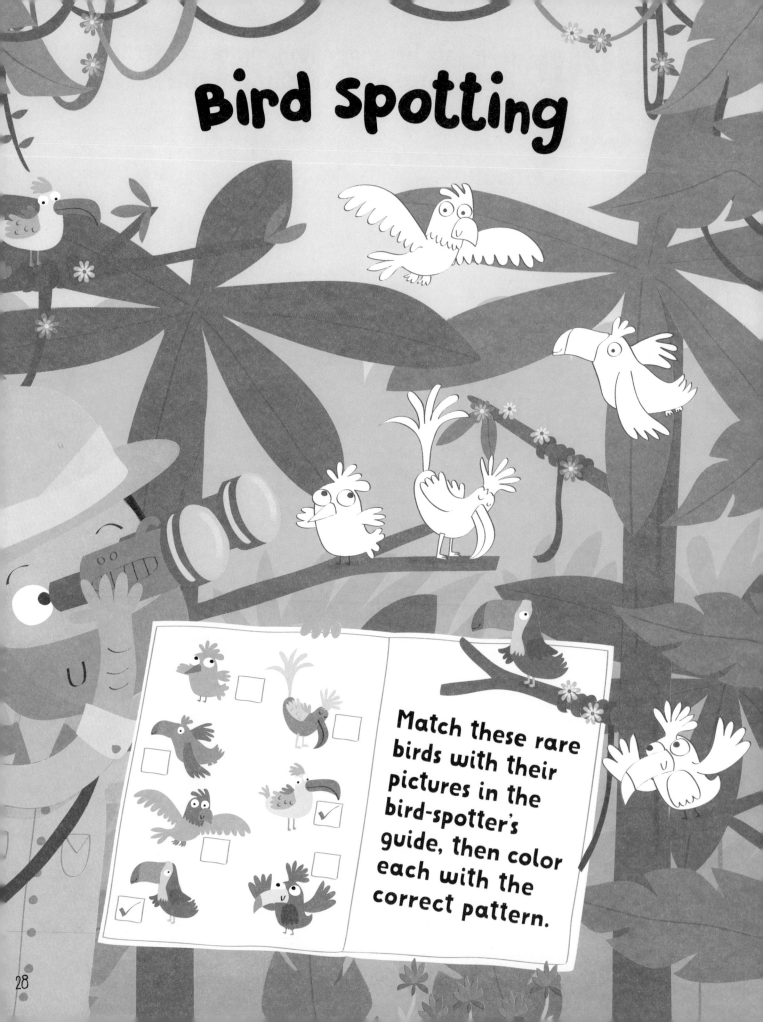

Match these rare birds with their pictures in the bird-spotter's guide, then color each with the correct pattern.

Bumble Jumble

Can you find Buzz? He's the only bee not part of a pair!

Odd robot out

Oops! There's a problem at the robot factory. Can you spot the robot that doesn't match?

A B C

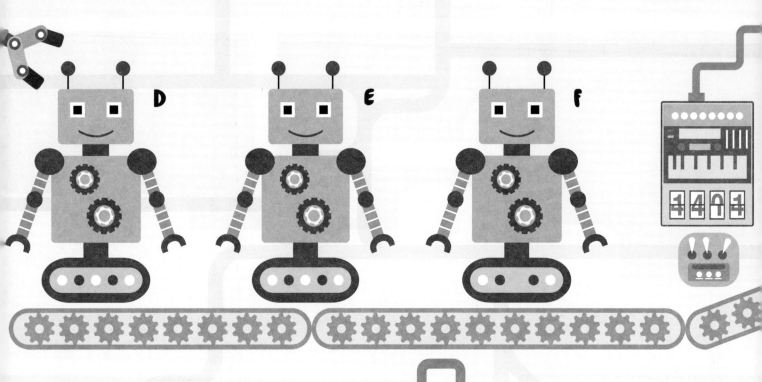

D E F

Lost in space

Astronaut Aiden has forgotten where he parked his spaceship. Starting from Aiden, follow the arrows by the number of squares marked on each arrow to find the ship.

Start

Aiden

Example

find and squeak

START

FINISH

Ginger the cat has lost her favorite toy!
Guide her through the maze to find it.

32

Dotty dress

Connect the dots to find out what's on the runway at this year's fashion show.

Then color in my new outfit!

Brave cave explorers

This creepy cave is full of letters!

```
B W T B R S T
T S M I O O Z E L Y H D S
S M E L L T W A E D I S P I D E R
W K U F E H D R A M X G A R V
W G C V I N C R E E P Y Q
W S C A R E K D B P G
H O W L D H R G R
W E Q F N I E
B S T R P
B A T
S
```

Find these words:

BAT   SCARE
BITE   SLIME
CREEPY   SLUG
DARK   SMELL
DRIP   SPIDER
HOWL   TOAD
OOZE   WEB

Costume calamity

Zap Man protects Super City from evil—but his costume is dirty! Which of these clean costumes is a replacement?

A

B

C

D

E

F

Who has been scrambled?

Copy each square into the correct section of the grid below to find out.

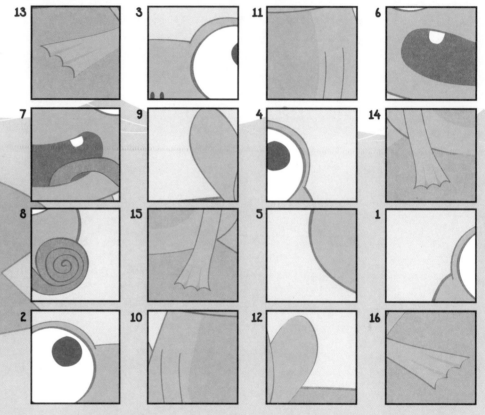

13	3	11	6
7	9	4	14
8	15	5	1
2	10	12	16

1	2	3	4
5	6	7	8
9	10	11	12
13	14	15	16

Pattern picker

Sequence 1

Sequence 2

Sequence 3

Sequence 4

Sequence 5

four friends

We do everything as a group! Can you find us standing together in the crowded grid?

40

Number web

Spinderella the spider loves to eat flies! Fit the numbers into the spaces in the grid so she can keep track of how many she's eaten.

43

48

258

354

426

2004

5886

6623

86564

6023568

9083157

The grid contains: 5, 0, 6, 6, 2, 3, 4

Dance away

Bobby pins

Apple

Dance shoes

Tights

Hairband

Leg Warmers

Purse

Comb

Water

Emily needs to pack a bag for her dance class. Look at
the things she needs for one minute, then turn the page
and see if you can remember them all!

Dotty Dessert

Connect the dots to reveal a delicious dessert!

Odd one out

Clara loves collecting, but there is one thing that doesn't belong in each of her collections. Draw a circle around each odd one out.

1

2

3

4

What am I?

Which six different animals have been put together to create me? Label each of my parts with the name of the animal it came from.

Head

Wings

Nose

Tongue

Tail

Body

45

secret formula

This experiment is nearly done! Which test tube will my secret formula end up in?

W   x   y   z

seaside slices

It's a lovely day to be by the sea, but this sunny snapshot has been cut into slices! Figure out the order it should be in, from left to right.

The correct order from left to right is:

H _ _ _ _ _ _ _ _

It's a jungle jumble!

Some of these amazing animals have never been seen before.

Which five creatures are not shown in the guide below?

Jewel journey

I've been given a new tiara for my birthday! Lead me to it by hopping across the gems in this order: ♦♦♦♦ Move forward, backward, up, or down.

START

FINISH

Go fish

How many fish can you find in this bowl?

magic words

Find all these
magical words
in Wanda's cauldron.

BOIL	MAGIC
BROOM	SNAIL
CAT	SPELL
FROG	TRICK
GREEN	POTION
HAT	SPIDER

```
      R L E B
    P O T I O N O S
  L U T G R E E N E P B P
  N A O T S B T I F E R G
  T B O I L F P R Y O L O N F
  U I M C R U S I A R L O R E
  S P O A L N C D M I M S
  T G L O T A K H E A P H
  M A G I C A F R
      H L E T
```

Best bubbles

Which mermaid has blown the most bubbles?

....

Shelley

Marina

Coral

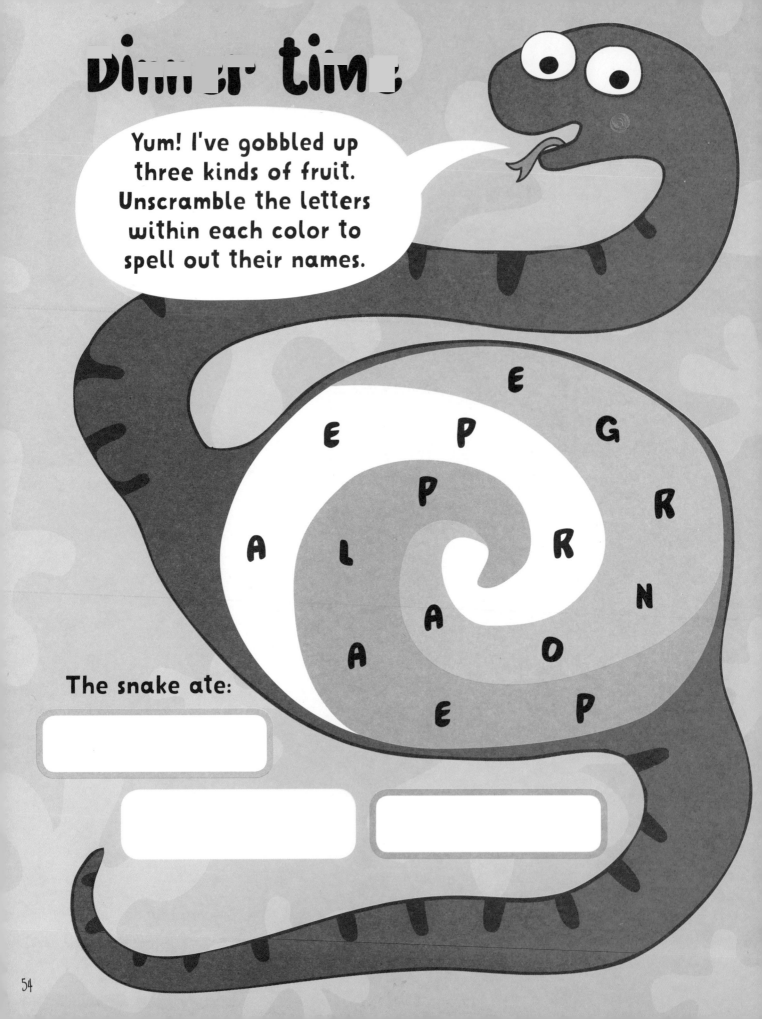

Dinner time

Yum! I've gobbled up three kinds of fruit. Unscramble the letters within each color to spell out their names.

The snake ate:

This mini-monster has a strange name:

MELLIFANGO

How many words can you make from it?

Write them all here.

1 ....
2 ....
3 ....
4 ....
5 ....
6 ....
7 ....
8 ....
9 ....
10 ....

11 ....
12 ....
13 ....
14 ....
15 ....
16 ....
17 ....
18 ....
19 ....
20 ....

How did you do?

0-5 words:
Shrunken brain!
6-10 words:
Monstrous mind!

11-15 words:
Scary smarty-pants!
16+ words:
Ghastly genius!

Bug hotel

Yikes! This room is full of creepy crawlies! How many times can you find the word BUG? Write your answer in the picture frame.

Don't forget, it could be written forward, backward, up, down, and diagonally!

B	G	U	B	B	G
G	U	B	U	G	U
U	B	G	G	U	B
B	U	G	U	B	U
U	G	U	B	B	G
G	U	B	U	G	B

....

56

CHIMP CHALLENGE

These clever chimps have figured out how to reach the highest bananas. Figure out what number is on each chimp by adding up the numbers on the two chimps immediately below.

Double Dance

These dancers are getting ready for the opening night!
Spot 10 differences in the bottom picture.

58

Super Spotting

It's playtime in the jungle, but which leopard has the most spots? Check off your answer!

A ☐
B ☐
C ☐
D ☐
E ☐
F ☐

Hide and seek

When no one is looking, the fairies come out to play! Can you figure out where each of these photos was taken and then find the fairies hiding in the garden?

Fairy cakes!

Pirate puzzle

One-Eyed William the pirate has lost his ship! One silhouette matches his drawing of it. Which one?

B

A

C

D

E

F

Ahoy there!

62

find a fossil

A new dinosaur fossil has been found. Connect the dots to reveal the skeleton, then name your dino!

This is my

.....................saurus!

63

slippy scarf

Everyone is making the most of the snow.
But which rabbit has left a scarf behind?
Follow the trails backward to find out.

speedy snails

Which snail will race to the finish first? Find a friend and each get a pencil. Choose a snail each, then put your pencils on the start line. Race your pencils down the tracks to see who can lead their snail to the finish line first! Ready, set, GO!

start A

start B

finish B

finish A

Digger repair

1   2   3   4   5   6   7   8   9   10

It's repair time on the building site! Each of the 10 spare parts belongs to one digger. Which two diggers don't have spares?

A   B   C   D   E   F   G   H   I   J   K   L

Big feast

- [ ] Bananas
- [ ] Apples
- [ ] Strawberries
- [ ] Pineapples
- [ ] Carrots
- [ ] Oranges

Gavin the gray bear loves all kinds of food. But what does he have the most of? Count the fruit in his dinner to find out.

Chase the cheetah

Quick!
Help us find the
way to the speedy
cheetah!

START

FINISH

Princess patterns

Princesses love to play number games!
Figure out the missing numbers in each row.

A: 14, ☐, 10, ☐, 6, 4

B: 5, ☐, 15, 20, ☐, 30

C: 1, 2, ☐, 8, ☐, 32

D: 1, 2, 4, 7, ☐, 16

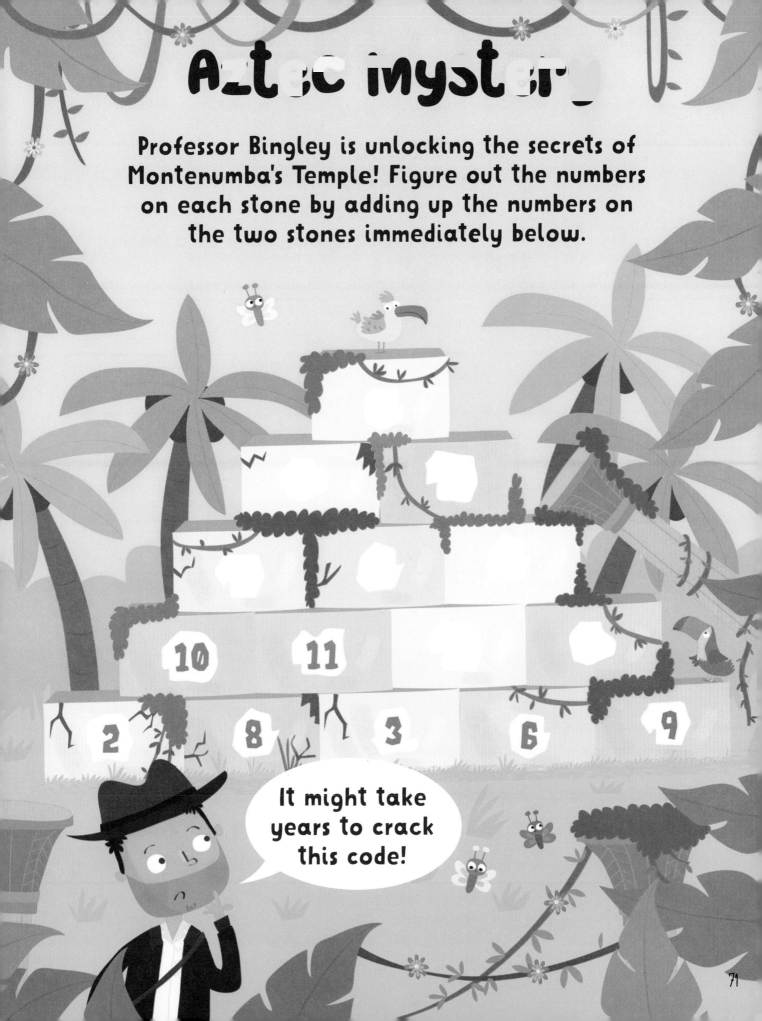

Aztec Mystery

Professor Bingley is unlocking the secrets of Montenumba's Temple! Figure out the numbers on each stone by adding up the numbers on the two stones immediately below.

It might take years to crack this code!

Lost ballet shoes!

Can you help me find a route to the stage that passes every shoe without crossing back over my path? Then circle the shoe that's not part of a pair.

START

FINISH

Something's wrong at the World Sports Championship.

Can you spot 12 things that aren't right in the stadium?

Duck Crossing

These ducks don't like to get their feet wet!
Find a way across the river, using the even-numbered stones
only and without going backwards.

Shoppers!

Find and check off all the items on the list.

- [ ] purple headphones
- [ ] light green shoes
- [ ] blue tie
- [ ] small orange handbag
- [ ] light blue backpack
- [ ] green scarf

77

Monster munchies

Find a path through the food
following the above order
You can move one square at a time,
up, down, and across, but not diagonally.

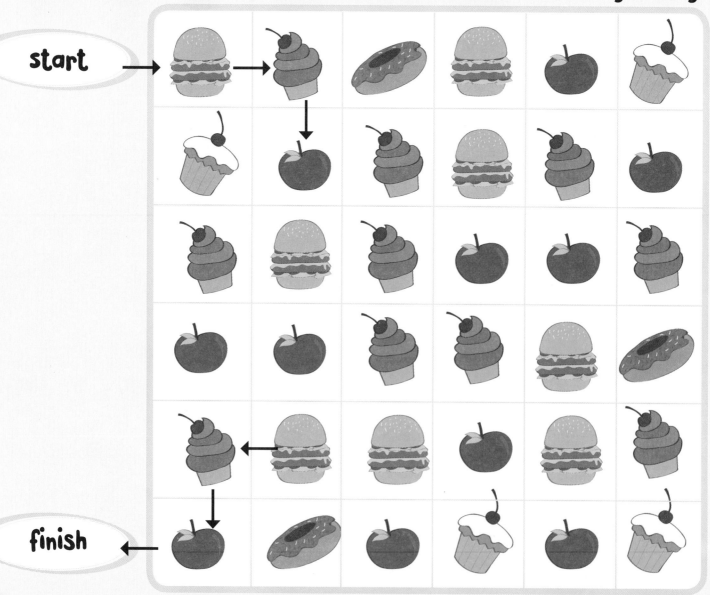

start

finish

Buried treasure

The most valuable
coin only appears once.
Which one is it?

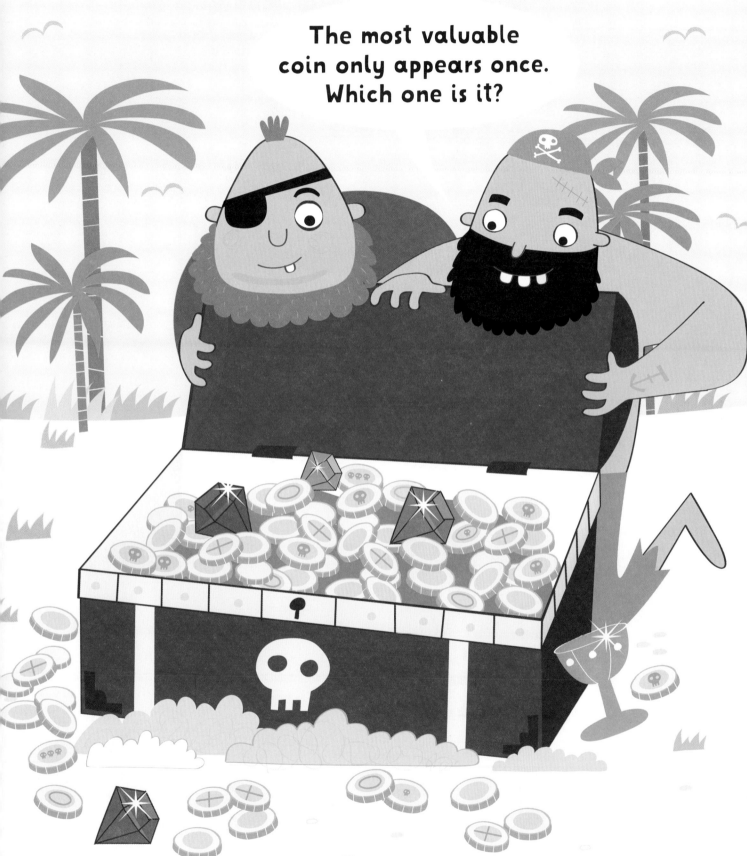

79

Bella ballerina
What will Bella wear today?
Find the dress that matches her description.

I want a dress with a bow. It should have spots. No stripes. I want some red on it. Can the dress have a belt, too?

castle copy

King Norbert's castle has been smashed in a big battle. Rebuild it by copying one square at a time, using the numbers to help you.

3	7	2	4
1	10	5	11
9	8	12	6

1	2	3	4
5	6	7	8
9	10	11	12

Dot to-dot du!

Join the dots to reveal some wild haircuts.

Plane trails

Follow the trails behind each plane to spell the name of the countries they're flying to.

Justin's bedroom

Justin's bedroom is **SO** messy, he can't find his favorite toys and clothes! Can you?

Check off the items as you find them.

- 9 pens
- 7 toy cars
- 6 action figures
- 5 dinosaurs and prehistoric reptiles
- 4 pairs of shoes
- 2 toy helicopters
- 1 football

Robot xt-003

Circle five parts that are missing
on this robot's right side.

which way?

Which route should I take
to park the tractor
in the barn?

A   B   C

Baker Gallery

Francis Baker is painting fakes of famous paintings, but he's not very good. Spot one mistake in each of his fakes.

Whale maze

Ben Barracuda has been accidentally swallowed by the whale.
Show him a way out of the whale's mouth so he can swim free.

finish

start

furgetful freddy!

Where is Freddy's car?
It's slightly different from all the other models.

90

Crowded bus

 30 MAX

SCHOOL BUS

 30 MAX

Mason wants to get on the school bus, but there are only 30 seats. Count the children already aboard to see if there is room for him.

Which weather?

Fog   Sun   Ice   Wind   Snow   Rain

Draw lines to match each item with
the right weather.

93

Purr-fect match

Match each white cat to the black cat
which has the same pattern.

Departures

DESTINATION	ANSWERS
S I P A R	
H N A G S N W I T O	
M O R E	
C O M O W S	
N L N O D O	
B U L I N D	

Unscramble each word to find out where each plane is flying. Use these stamps as clues if you need to!

PARIS FRANCE

LONDON

MOSCOW

ROME

WASHINGTON

IRELAND

Dance-off

Can you figure out which dance move comes next?

Draw your answers below

Owl match

Tonight the trees are full of owls. Find all the matching pairs.

castle confusion

My castle is missing five pieces! Compare both sides, then find five parts that are missing from the right-hand side.

Bug hunt

100

Space Search

Can you help the starship find all
these words on the asteroids?
Look up, down, and across.

B R K C Q O O Z O V C A I O L N A C X V
V V E N U S M M S A T U R N S U B O C G
B A S Z T A A A E P O F G Y Z L V M S W
V C R S P A C E D J G X F U H H S E R B
Y P Z W E P F J L C H D M Y B T N T M U
O Q L M D V J P G X D E M Y V R E I O E
A U H S C F F L O V R U D P J A D Q O Q
V R T R R J D A G M U P Z W F E W U N L
E A Q A B I J N S V B L R E T J Y D Q H
H N U M R D W E Q N E P T U N E J S Z A
R U P R K P V T E P Q R Z B Y Q U U W J
H S J U P I T E R L V X S T A R A I H O

- COMET
- EARTH
- JUPITER
- MARS
- MOON
- NEPTUNE
- PLANET
- SATURN
- SPACE
- STAR
- URANUS
- VENUS

Toy box

We always stick together! Can you find us sitting in this exact order in the toy box?

Dragon day

1

2

3

4

5

6

7

8

9

10

Mama Dragon's baby is hatching! List the pictures in the right order to show the baby breaking free of his egg.

Egg _ _ _ _ _ _ _ _ _ _ Dragon

sail away

It's a beautiful day aboard the cruise ship! But can you find 9 differences in its reflection?

Ready to rock!

Which rock-star pieces fit into the concert scene? Write the letters in the spaces.

Butterfly beauties

How many matching pairs of butterflies can you spot?

There are ___ pairs of butterflies.

sky high

Animal Halves

Use the word parts from the bottom of the page to finish the zoo signs!

GOR_____

_____HANT

___KEY

SK____

__ON

___TURE

BO___

SCOR_____

LI

PION

VUL

MON

ELEP

UNK

ILLA

AR

Time out

Can you re-build Princess Ticktock's
grandfather clock from the broken parts?

Top __ __ __ __ __ __ bottom

Midnight magic

Where do all the missing pieces fit in this sleepy scene?

Missing Music

Which cello is mine? Match the silhouette to find out!

The instrument that matches is

Creepy Creatures

Oops! I've magically mixed up these six creatures. Help me figure out what they were so I can change them back.

The creatures are:

1 ....

2 ....

3 ....

4 ....

5 ....

6 ....

flushed away

START

Oops! Princess Jinx has dropped her favorite ring! Find a path through the plumbing to return it to her.

FINISH

which bike?

Read the descriptions to figure out whose bike is whose!

MY BIKE IS NOT BLUE!

MY BIKE DOES NOT HAVE A BASKET!

MY BIKE HAS A BLACK SEAT AND NO BASKET!

Jenny

Alicia

Emily

fairground fun

Fill in the blank spaces on the big wheel so that each pair of numbers joined through the middle adds up to 16.

Help us crack the safe! fit the List of numbers into the grid below. The numbers in the red circles are the code!

Robber rats

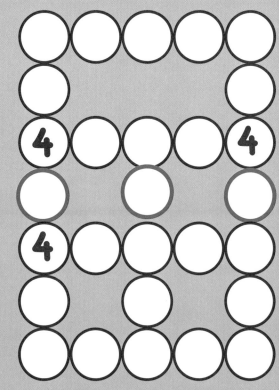

15798
24598
32816
40134
46743
2540423
8743306

flower power

It's springtime in the park. Find these three special flowers in the colorful display:

Snip Snap

Who's new at the zoo? Connect the dots to find out, and colour them in!

Answers

p4 - MATH

p5

p6

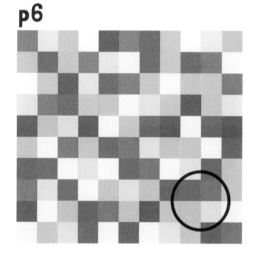

p8 - 3 green, 2 orange, 3 blue, 2 pink, 2 purple

p9

p10
6 + 6 = 12, 15 − 5 = 10, 6 + 3 = 9
12 − 5 = 7, 4 + 3 = 7

p11 – **C**6

p12 - 13

p14 - PLANET EARTH!

p15
AUSTRALIA   GERMANY
BRAZIL   MEXICO
CANADA   JAMAICA
ENGLAND   FRANCE

p16
SLOW and FAST
SHORT and TALL
LIGHT and HEAVY
WET and DRY
HOT and COLD
YOUNG and OLD
DIRTY and CLEAN

p17 - Slice 1 = 8. More than one way to make the other slices add up to 8.

p18

p19

p20-21 - The monster ordered **CAKE**.
You need to draw:
3 muffins, 3 cupcakes, 4 cookies

p22-23

p24-25

p26 - Shadow **D**

p27

p28

p29

p30 - Robot **F**

p31 - Spaceship **C**

p32

p33 - Your dot-to-dot should reveal a fashionable mini dress!

122

p34

p35 - Suit E

p36 - 37

p38

p39

1 2 3
4 5

p40

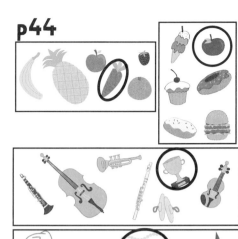

p41

2 5 8   6
8   0   9
4 8   2 0 0 4
6 6 2 3   8
5   3   3
4 2 6   1   5
4   8 6 5 6 4
7

p43 - Your dot-to-dot should reveal an ice cream sundae!

p44

p45 - Head – lion; tail –scorpion; body – gorilla; tongue – snake; nose – elephant; wings – bat

p46 - Test tube X

p47 - H, C, F, B, G, D, A, I, E

p48 - 49

p50

p51 - 16 fish

123

p52

p53 - Coral blew 34 bubbles. Marina blew 19 bubbles. Shelley blew 15 bubbles. Coral blew the most bubbles.

p54 - ORANGE, APPLE, PEAR.

p55 - You could have:
AM, GO, IF, MA, NO, ON, AGE, FIN, FOG, ILL, LEG, LOG, MAN, MEN, OIL, FALL, FAME, FELL, FLAG, FLEA, FLOG, FOAM, FOIL, GAME, GOLF, GONE, LEAF, LIFE, LIME, LOAF, LONG, MALL, MEAL, MILE, MOLE, NAME, ANGEL, FLAME, FLING, GNOME, FLAMINGO.

p56 - The word BUG appears 22 times.

p57

48
20 28
8 12 16
3 5 7 9
1 2 3 4 5

p58

p59 - Leopard F with 12 spots.

p60-61

p62 - Ship D

p63 - Your dot-to-dot should reveal a giant dino skeleton.

p64 - Rabbit E

p66 - C and H don't have spares.

p67
6 bananas
5 apples
7 strawberries
5 pineapples
6 carrots
6 oranges

Strawberries are his favorite.

p68
A 14
B 21
C 11
D 15
E 05
F 12

p69

p70

A 14, 12, 10, 8, 6, 4
B 5, 10, 15, 20, 25, 30
C 1, 2, 4, 8, 16, 32
D 1, 2, 4, 7, 11, 16

p71

```
            85
        41    44
      21   20   24
    10   11   9   15
   2   8   3   6   9
```

p72

p73

p74-75

p76

p77

p78

p79

p80

p82 – Your dot-to-dot should reveal one spiky hairstyle and one very tall hairpiece with a bow!

125

p83
1 Australia
2 Switzerland
3 Madagascar

p88

p90

p84 - 85

p91 - There are 29 children, so there is 1 space left for Mason.

p92 – Greensnot won with 15 fish.

p93 - Sun – sunglasses; rain – umbrella; wind – kite; snow – sled; fog – flashlight; ice – ice skates

p94

p86

p89

p87 – Track C

126

p95

1. PARIS
2. WASHINGTON
3. ROME
4. MOSCOW
5. LONDON
6. DUBLIN

p96 - 97

p98

1, 11	7, 10
2, 6	8, 19
3, 15	9, 17
4, 18	12, 16
5, 14	13, 20

p99

p100 - There are 30 outlines.

p101

p102

p103

8, 2, 6, 1, 4, 3, 9, 5, 7, 10

p104

p105

p106-107 - There are 10 butterfly pairs.

p108

A–3	D–6
B–5	E–1
C–4	F–2

p109

ELEP-HANT	MON-KEY
GOR-ILLA	SCOR-PION
LI-ON	BO-AR
SK-UNK	VUL-TURE

p110   F, C, E, B, A, D

p111

1, E	5, A
2, G	6, B
3, F	7, D
4, H	8, C

p112 - Silhouette D

p113

duck	skunk
rat	spider
octopus	frog

p114

127

p115
Jenny has bike B
Alicia has bike **C**
Emily has bike A

p116

p117

p118-119

p120 - Your dot-to-dot should reveal a crocodile!

TOTALLY AMAZING MAZES

BEFORE YOU GET STARTED ...

Every maze has a START and a FINISH. Find a route through to solve it!

If you see a dead end or blockage in a maze, don't give up! Just turn back and find another path.

You might have to avoid things on the way, like this scary monster!

You might have to catch things, like these escaped zombies.

134

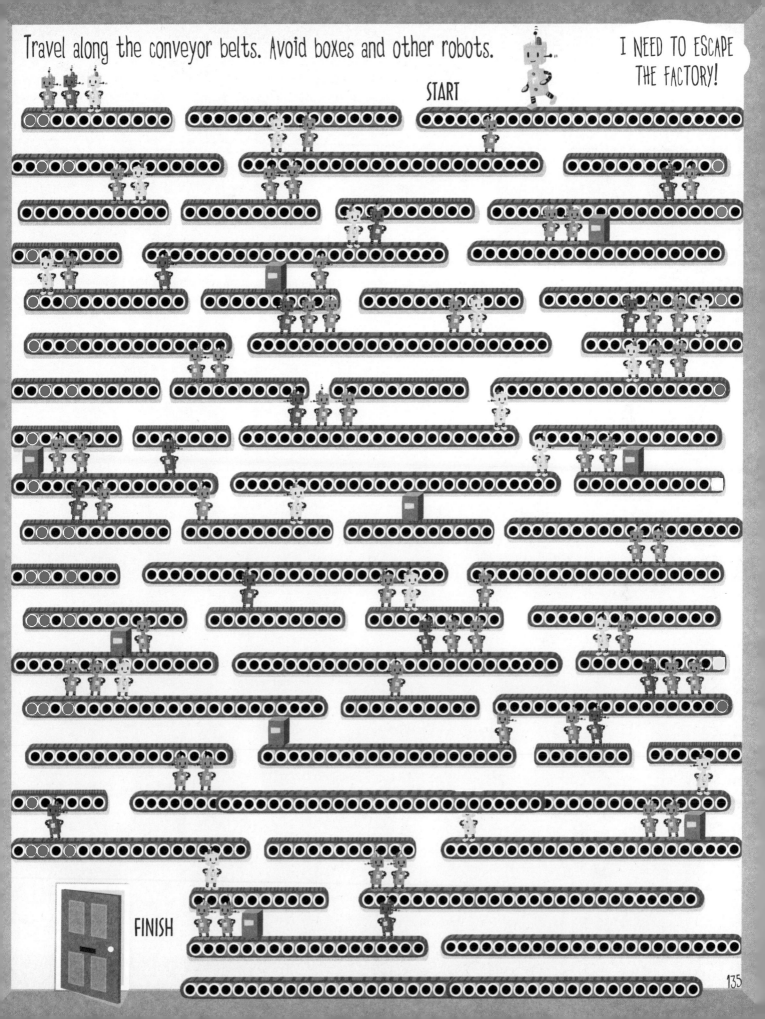

Travel along the conveyor belts. Avoid boxes and other robots.

START

I NEED TO ESCAPE THE FACTORY!

FINISH

Help Little fish escape Octopus's tangly arms.

START

FINISH

Mole can't find his friend.

START

FINISH

I'm down here!

138

Help Ella find the way between the umbrellas to her matching umbrella.

START

FINISH

Twelve teachers have been turned into monsters in a science experiment disaster. Collect the bottle of antidote from the science lab ... just don't bump into any monsters on the way!

START

FINISH

22+14

The beach is a dangerous place for a little turtle.
Help Rocky find a route between the sand dunes to reach the ocean safely.

START

Snappy crabs!

Hungry seagulls!

Deadly driftwood!

FINISH

FINISH

145

This car isn't ready to be crushed. Drive it out of the wrecking yard.

START

FINISH

147

Meet Stunt Pilot Penguin, about to perform another death-defying trick. Follow the vapor trails to land him safely.

START

Way to go,
Stunt Pilot Penguin!

FINISH

Take a tour of Thrillville Theme Park.

START

150

FINISH

Help the caterpillar munch its way along
a trail of leaves to its friend.

START

FINISH

Use the empty ladders to get Roofer Rob to the leaky roof.

FINISH

Roofer Rob

START

153

FINISH

155

Slimy wants to meet Shelly for lunch. Help him avoid all the creepy-crawlies on the way.

START

FINISH

Take the escaped mummy back to where it belongs.
Don't scare any tourists on the way!

Avoid the knots in this sneaker tangle!

START

FINISH

Quick, you've got a plane to catch! Jump in this taxi to the airport. Don't run any red lights along the way.

START

FINISH

Race the mouse to the attic and get through the mouse hole to escape the cat. Use stairs, ladders, and open doors to get there.

FINISH

START

163

FINISH

WATCH OUT
FOR DEADLY
RATTLESNAKES!

START

Carefully climb Cactus Canyon ...

164

Deep in the jungle, the explorers are hoping
to catch sight of the rare giant panda.
Travel between the bamboo branches.

START

FINISH

167

Ride the rollercoaster. Just avoid the other cars!

START

FINISH

Can you smell toasting marshmallows? Find your way to the campfire.

START

FINISH

Follow the snow trails. There's only one way down!

START

FINISH

171

FINISH

START

Unlock the safe to get your hands on the world's largest diamond.

Loop between the popsicles for a sweet reward!

START

FINISH

Nee-nah! Nee-nah! Drive the fire crew to the rescue!

START

Just don't crash into anything on the way.

HELP!

The fire's this way!

FINISH

FINISH

START

Which station shall we stop by today?

Dinosaur Square!

START

FINISH

DINOSAUR SQUARE

Guide Curtis the cat through the streets to his friends.

START

FINISH

Princess Polly wants to climb the tower and see the WHOLE kingdom.

The view's great up here!

FINISH

Guide the seahorse between the seaweed to his true love.

START

FINISH

REALLY BRAVE

FINISH

TOTALLY AWESOME!

GETTING BRAVER

BEGINNER

START

Take the ski lift to the highest mountain.
You can only travel along cables
without another car on them.

191

194

Travel over each blue ghost to zap them all on the way to the end of the level.

195

START

100 POINTS!

FINISH

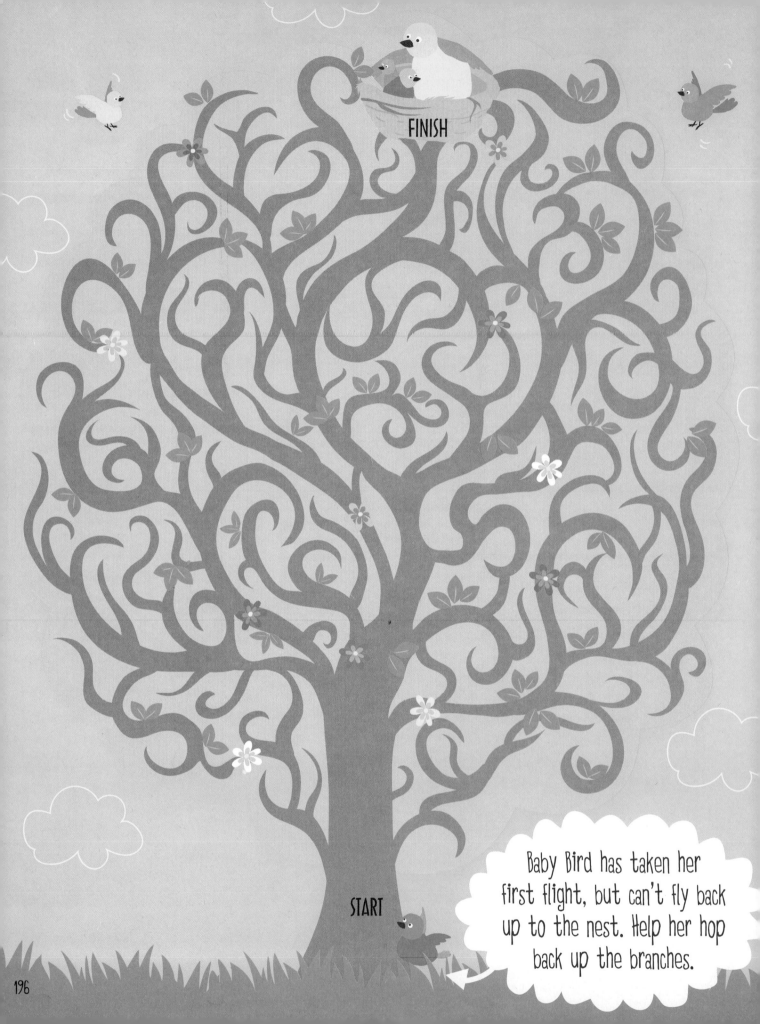

FINISH

START

Baby Bird has taken her first flight, but can't fly back up to the nest. Help her hop back up the branches.

196

Edge through the hedges to the magical fountain.

START

FINISH

202

203

204

START

FINISH

Mommy, where are you? We're hungry!

205

Dodge the craters and get the moon buggy back to the spaceship.

START

WATCH OUT FOR ALIENS!

Seal feeding starts soon. If you're really quick, you can visit the tigers, zebras, shark, and raccoons on the way!

SEAL FEEDING AT 2PM

START

FINISH

START

Rescue truck

A car has broken down and the roads are jammed with traffic!
Find a way through for the rescue truck.

Broken-down car

FINISH

Monkey has lost his troop ...

START ➞

FINISH

START

Mason's lost his red kite! Find a route between the other kites to catch it.

Help Mick row the boat to dry land without touching any 'gators.

START

Alligator Alley

218

FINISH

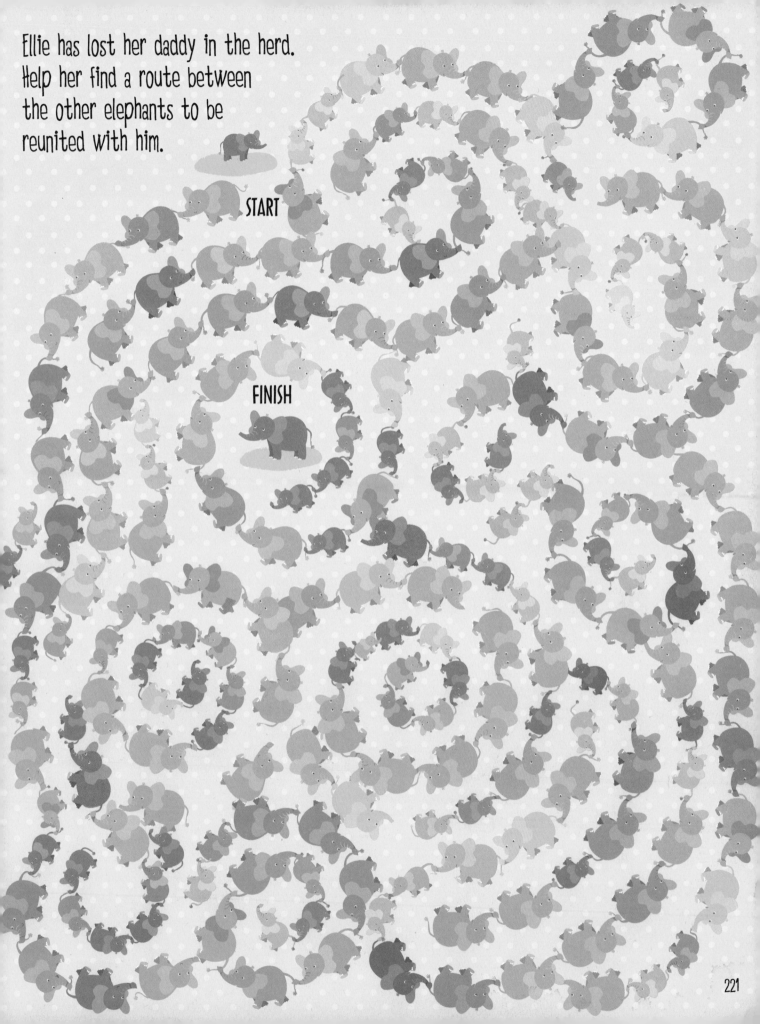

Ellie has lost her daddy in the herd. Help her find a route between the other elephants to be reunited with him.

START

FINISH

221

START

Ben's only got ten minutes left in the Adventure Play Park. Pass every red flag to visit each activity and get him to the exit ... Mom's waiting!

FINISH

222

223

Help One-eyed Violet hop across the pirate ships to reach the treasure.

START

224

FINISH

As long as the bus driver picks up all six children on the way to school, everyone will be on time for class.

START

SCHOOL

FINISH

225

START

Avoid the seaweed tangle and guide Marissa the mermaid home.

HOME

FINISH

228

It's the rally in the valley!
Skid 'n' slide to the finish line.

START

FINISH

230

START

Bring Frankenstein's monster to life
with this bubbling pink potion.

I'm alive!

FINISH

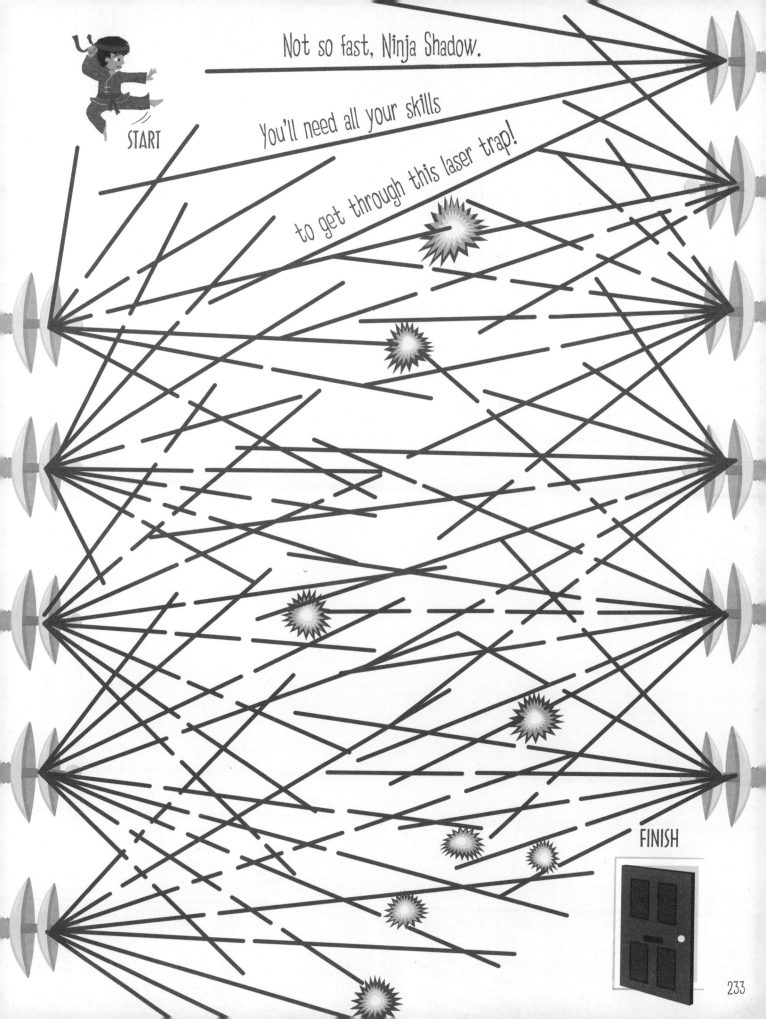

Not so fast, Ninja Shadow.

You'll need all your skills

to get through this laser trap!

START

FINISH

233

Make the most of your safari trip and see every animal along the way!
Watch out for other safari vehicles.

START

FINISH

235

There are lots of roadworks and traffic jams today! Can you find a way home?

START

FINISH

237

Mega Blob and his beastly buddies are taking over the city.
There's only one thing for it ... RUN!

START

FINISH

238

FINISH

Help Danny find the eraser in his backpack.

START

FINISH

Help the woodsman find his log piles.
He's going home to build a toasty fire!

START

FINISH

243

244

FINISH

I ♥

START

FINISH

SOLUTIONS

Page 134

Page 135

Page 136

Page 137

Page 138

Page 139

Pages 140-141

Page 142

Page 143

Pages 144-145

Page 146

Page 147

Pages 148-149

Pages 150-151

Page 152

Page 153

Pages 154-155

Page 156

Page 157

Page 158

Page 159

Pages 160-161

Page 162

Page 163

Page 164

Page 165

Pages 166-167

Page 168

Page 169

Page 170

Page 171

Pages 172-173

Page 174

Page 175

Page 176

Page 177

252   Pages 178-179

Page 180

Page 181

Page 182   Page 183   Pages 184-185

Page 186   Page 187   Page 188   Page 189

Page 190   Page 191   Page 192   Page 193

Page 194   Page 195   Page 196   Page 197

Page 198   Page 199   Page 200   Page 201

Page 202   Page 203   Page 204   Page 205

Pages 206-207   Page 208   Page 209

Page 210   Page 211   Pages 212-213

Page 214

Page 215

Page 216

Page 217

Pages 218-219

Page 220

Page 221

Page 222

Page 223

Page 224

Page 225

Page 226

Page 227

Page 228

Page 229

Page 230

Page 231

Page 232

Page 233

Pages 234-235

Page 236

Page 237

Page 1238

Page 239

Pages 240-241

Page 242

Page 243

Pages 244-245

Page 246

Page 247

Pages 248-249